DATE DUE MAR		
FEB 7 1975	DE 1 '81	JAN 2 3 198
9/6 2 2 1976	DE 21 '81	FEB 5 198
FEB 2 1977	MR 3 '82	MAR 4 1986
MAR 9 1977	DE 20 '82	SEP 3 8 1986
SEP 1 4 1977	OCT 5 '83	OCT 2 3 1986
SEP 2 2 1978	OC 26 '8	NOV 1 1 198
FEB 5 980	MAY 2 1 1984	FEB 3 1987
MAR 1 8 1980	OCT 8 198	NOV 3 1987
MAR 2 7 1980	NOV 2 8 198	NOV 1 7 1987
MAY 1 1980	OCT 2 2 198	DEC 1 1987
MR 4 '8 MY 26 '8	NOV 0 5 198	JAN 4
MR 19 '8 MY 27 '8	NOV 2 7 198	MAY 18 APR 30

To Pierre Wormser
From his godmother
For all his children to come

About the Book

Pierre was lonely, and he was often hungry. How he dreamed of roasting sausage over the open fire! So Pierre and his mother and father saved their money and bought a piglet. The piglet would grow fat and make fine sausage. Pierre named the piglet Marcel, and he took good care of his pet. The little boy was not lonely now, for Marcel was his friend.

In this charming and suspenseful story, which takes place in the Périgord region of France, Pierre learns some surprising facts about truffles. Knobby, brown mushroom-like truffles are hard to find because they grow underground, usually around the roots of oak trees. Truffles are used in French goose liver pate, world-famous pate de foie gras, as well as in many other delectable dishes. They are a rare and tasty treat! People love to eat truffles and they will pay a lot of money for them. Pigs love to eat them too, and they know how to find them and dig them up.

But what about Marcel? Will he be made into sausage? And how does he come to be called "the Truffle Pig"?

Children will love reading the story of Pierre and Marcel, and they will delight in Kurt Wiese's wonderfully expressive illustrations.

The Truffle Pig

by Claire Huchet Bishop
and Kurt Wiese

COWARD, McCANN & GEOGHEGAN, INC.   NEW YORK

A Break-of-Day Book

Ever since 1928, when Wanda Gág's *Millions of Cats* appeared ("a landmark of children's literature," says May Hill Arbuthnot, in *Children's Reading in the Home*, which "marked the beginning of a spectacular development of picture stories,") Coward, McCann & Geoghegan has been publishing books of high quality for young readers.

Now, a new group of easy-to-read stories, known as Break-of-Day Books, appears under the colophon shown above — a rooster crowing in the sunrise — taken from Wanda Gág's illustrations for *Tales from Grimm* and *More Tales from Grimm.*

Though the language used in Break-of-Day Books is deliberately kept as clear and as simple as possible, the stories are *not* written in a controlled vocabulary. And while chosen to be within the grasp of readers in the primary grades, their content is far-ranging and varied enough to captivate children who have just begun crossing the momentous threshhold into the world of books.

Text copyright © 1971 by Claire Huchet Bishop

Illustrations copyright © 1971 by Kurt Wiese

Library of Congress Catalog Card Number: 70-132619

PRINTED IN THE UNITED STATES OF AMERICA
06209

Once upon a time

there was a boy named Pierre.

He lived with his father and mother

on a small farm,

in a country called France.

Pierre was lonely,

and he was often hungry.

The family was very poor.

"If only we had a pig!" Papa said.

"A pig, we can never afford.

But we might buy a piglet

and raise it," Mama suggested.

"Right you are!" Papa cried.

"Then, come winter and bad weather,

we could always have plenty to eat."

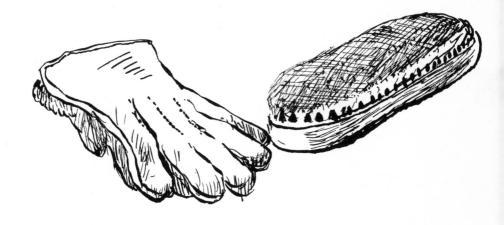

"And could I roast a sausage on a fork
over the open fire?" Pierre asked.
"Of course!" Papa said.
"And we shall sell the pig's skin
for leather goods
and the bristles for brushes.
Not a bit of a pig
is ever wasted."

Yes, indeed, to buy a piglet,
that was the thing to do!
And they began to save
as much as they could,
each time they sold their hens' eggs.

Pierre saved his money, too.

Every morning he went to fetch firewood

for Madame Marcel,

their old neighbor.

Pierre told Madame Marcel about the piglet.

Madame Marcel gave Pierre some pennies
and a piggy bank.
She said, "When it is full,
you smash it,
and then you get your money."
Pierre thanked her.
He put the pennies in the slot.

Pierre loved to shake his piggy bank.
It spoke to him of sausage
roasted on a fork
over the open fire.

13

Papa and Mama kept saving
as much as they could
on their egg money.
They put their savings
in a woolen sock.

One morning Papa said,

"This is the big day!

We are going to the market

to buy a piglet."

Mama brought out the woolen sock.

Pierre took his piggy bank with him.

What a noisy place the market was!

Sheep cried, baa-baa,

goats, may-may,

chickens, cluck-cluck,

ducks, quack-quack,

pigs, oink-oink,

geese, hiss-hiss,

cows, moo-moo,

horses, neigh-neigh,

donkeys, hee-haw,

and roosters, cock-a-doodle-do!

And the merchants shouted their wares,

"See my wonderful cabbages!

Buy my tender lettuce!

Look at my beautiful carrots!"

Pierre wondered where the piglets were.

Suddenly he stopped in front of a stall.

There was something there

he had never seen before —

a big heap of ugly-looking

small dark-brown knobs.

What could they be?

"Truffles! Truffles!

Smooth, perfect truffles!

Who wants truffles?" the merchant chanted.

"Where do they grow?" Pierre asked.

"Underground only, my boy."

"Truffles are very expensive, aren't they?"

said Pierre, looking at the price tag.

"They taste wonderful.

Rich people pay a lot of money

for truffles, my boy."

"Pierre! Pierre!"

Pierre ran in the direction of Mama's voice.

Ah, here were the piglets!

Papa and Mama were talking

with the merchant about one of them.

It was tiny, with a lovely pink color.

It looked very bright.

Pierre liked it at once.

"Your price is too high
for such a piglet,"
Papa argued.

"It will grow," the merchant answered.

"Give us a break," Papa said.

"I have come down as much
as I could already,"
the merchant grumbled.

"Please!" Mama pleaded.

"We do not have quite enough

to meet your price."

"Sorry, madame, it's take it or leave it."

Papa and Mama looked at each other.

They shook their heads

and started to walk away.

"Wait!" Pierre cried.

He made a big swing with his arm

and opened his hand.

Bing! Bang! Crash went the piggy bank

down on the stone pavement!

They counted the money.

There was just enough

to make up what they needed

to meet the merchant's price.

Papa lifted the piglet
and put it in a bag.
"Please, let me carry it," Pierre said.
"It's *my* piglet."

Pierre called the piglet Marcel.

He told Madame Marcel

he had named it for her.

She was very pleased.

Pierre took good care of Marcel.
Every day he brought him his food,
cleaned his sty,
brushed him, and talked to him.
Soon Marcel grunted loudly
each time he saw Pierre.
Pierre was not lonely anymore.

Marcel followed Pierre everywhere.

Together they called on Madame Marcel.

She said, "You look like

a very bright pig, Marcel.

I'm not surprised.

You were named for me!

Too bad I cannot treat you

to some truffles!

How about some acorns?"

Marcel liked the acorns.

Pierre had chocolate custard.

Marcel grew and grew.

He became a handsome pig.

One day Papa said,
"Pierre, soon you will be able
to roast a sausage
on a fork over the open fire!
That pig is fat enough.
Tomorrow is the time."
What? Marcel? Pierre's friend?
It could not be!

Pierre ran to the sty.

He put his arms around Marcel
and whispered,
"We shall run away, you and I.
Tonight, together!"

When evening came, Pierre said,
"I am going to take Marcel
for a walk."
He gave Mama a big hug,
and he kissed Papa, too.
He put on his cap
and out he went.

E
Bis

Farther and farther
they tramped on into the woods,
farther than they had ever gone before.

Suddenly Marcel stopped,
sniffed, groaned, grunted.
He jumped around wildly.
He began to dig with all his might
at the foot of an oak tree.
"Marcel! Marcel! Come on!" Pierre begged.
The pig paid no attention.
Pierre tried to pull him away.
But Marcel would not budge.
He dug and dug, furiously.

All at once, out of the hole
rolled a dark-brown ugly knob.
Pierre shrieked and threw himself down on it
before Marcel could swallow it.

A truffle!

Like the expensive ones Pierre had seen,

months before, at the market!

Pierre ran all the way back home.

Marcel ran, too.

He wanted the truffle Pierre held

hidden in his hand.

It smelled like strawberries.

Papa and Mama were on the doorstep.

"Where have you been?" they shouted.

"Look! Look!" Pierre cried.

And he opened his hand.

"A truffle! Where did you get it?"

"Marcel found it. He dug it out."

"Good heavens!" Mama shrieked.

"A truffle pig!"

"A truffle pig! Whoopee!" Papa yelled.

And he took hold of Mama's

and Pierre's hands,

and they began to dance around Marcel.

"From now on," Papa said,

"not a bristle of this pig

shall be touched!"

"He will be our family breadwinner,"

Mama added.

"How?" Pierre asked.

"He will hunt for truffles,

and we shall sell them,"

Papa explained.

"Right," Mama said.

"People do not know where

truffles grow underground.

Only pigs, smart pigs, do."

"Like Marcel!" Pierre shouted.

He was very happy.

Every morning Marcel, Pierre, Mama, and Papa

went to the woods.

Marcel hunted for truffles.

Pierre, Papa, and Mama

put them in a bag.

Sometimes Papa gave Marcel

a small piece of cheese.

Pierre let Marcel eat a truffle

once in a while.

He liked them so much!

Madame Marcel liked truffles, too.

Pierre brought her some.

She was pleased with Marcel's good fortune.

"I always knew he was

a very bright pig!" she said.

Every week Papa, Mama and Pierre
went to the market.
They sold truffles.
Soon they had many, many customers.
Pierre was never hungry anymore.
By and by they built a lovely house
with a huge fireplace.
Marcel had a new sty
with blue tiles and a pond.

Pierre invited Madame Marcel
for a celebration.
He roasted many a sausage on a fork
over the open fire — *beef* sausages only!
They tasted so good!

Marcel became very famous.

He was awarded first prize

in a nationwide

Truffle-Pig Contest.

From then on
Papa and Mama did not have to
go to market anymore.
Marcel went on truffle hunting
just for the fun of it.
There were always plenty of truffles
for Madame Marcel and for Pierre.
And more than enough
for his good friend, Marcel,
the truffle pig!

About the Author

Claire Huchet Bishop, raised and educated in France, is well known for her many children's books, some of them translated into several languages and singled out for awards. One of her stories, *The Five Chinese Brothers*, has long been a favorite of children around the world. The author's published works also include adult books, poetry, book reviews, and magazine articles.

For many years, Mrs. Bishop has been a lecturer for the NDEA Institutes and for the Danforth Foundation, here and in France. She makes her home both in New York City and in Paris.

About the Artist

Born in Germany, Kurt Wiese lived for a while in Manchuria, where he mastered the Chinese language and calligraphy. Later, in Australia, he began writing and drawing, in an attempt to record his impressions of the strange animals and scenery he saw there.

He has since become a very popular writer and illustrator of many outstanding children's books, including *The Five Chinese Brothers*, an earlier collaboration with Claire Huchet Bishop.

Mr. Wiese and his wife now live in Frenchtown, New Jersey.